The
Raindance

Written and Illustrated By Glenn McLernon

In Little Apple,
water was very dear.
For there was no rain:
for a week
or a month
or a year.

The leaves on the trees were crispy and dry.
The grass was brown and yellow.
The crops in the fields just would not grow.
It made the poor farmers cry.

"What can we do?" The people cried.
"We must have water to stay alive.
We must have water to wash things clean
and to make plants grow, as well you know."

"And we need water too."
Said Nora Nuff to Mrs C,
who loved a good old natter,
over a nice cup of tea.

So McNat, a friendly old cat,
who sometimes looked like a man with a hat,
went to his friend, old Bungie Boo,
who lived in a shed, that looked like a shoe.

"The people need our help."
Said McNat.
"But what can I do
in this funny old hat?"

So they thought and they thought.
Then they slept and they snored.
So what were they thinking
or were they just bored?

Bungie Boo's eyebrows went up!
and his eyes opened wide!
"I have, I have, I have it. " He cried.
"It's the best idea that has ever been tried. "

"So tell me this and tell me no more."
Said McNat, who was always good at keeping the score.
"Please tell me this big idea of yours. "

"Oh! It's simple, you see."
Said Bungie Boo.
"We'll have a raindance.
It'll be tickety boo."

"Wow!" Said McNat.
"Now why didn't I think of that?"
"We'll have a big night, a party
   and a bonfire too."

The big night came.

Bungie Boo was dressed
like a man of some ancient race
with flowers on his head
and paint on his face
and a big huge drum,
to beat out a hummmmm,
to call to the sky and make the rain come.

The people came
from the ends of the town.
Some were wearing
their dressing gowns.

Everyone came from far and wide.
They were hoping to make it rain for a while.

There was Mrs C and Nora Nuff
and Constable Crabbe
and Billy Buff.

Little babies, grannies and all,
they came with hope
that the rain might fall.

The people danced around the big fire
to the beat of the drum
with everyone chanting
some deep humm, humm, humm.

They were shaking their rain-sticks,
a magical sound.
They were hoping the rain
would fall to the ground.

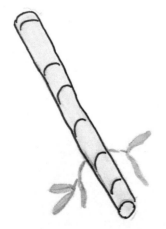

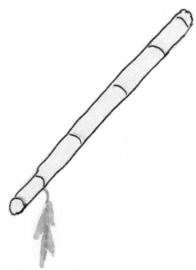

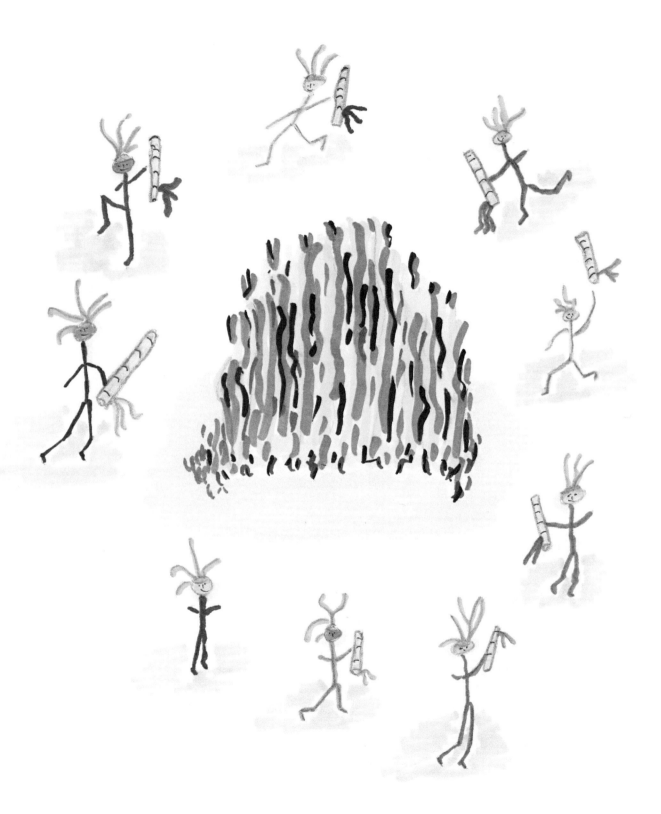

Old Cloudius looked down
on the dusty old town.
He was shaking his head
with a funny old frown.

"Oh sorry," he said,
"my apologies instead.
I forgot to make it rain
on your heads."

The people kept dancing
around the big fire

and while McNat
looked down from a tree,
a squirrel crept up
and said "hee, hee, hee."

And Nora Nuff and Mrs C
were having a natter
and a nice cup of tea.

Old Cloudius
was wondering what to do.
He had some spare clouds
somewhere, he knew.

He searched in his night sky.
He searched in his day
but couldn't remember
where he hid them away.

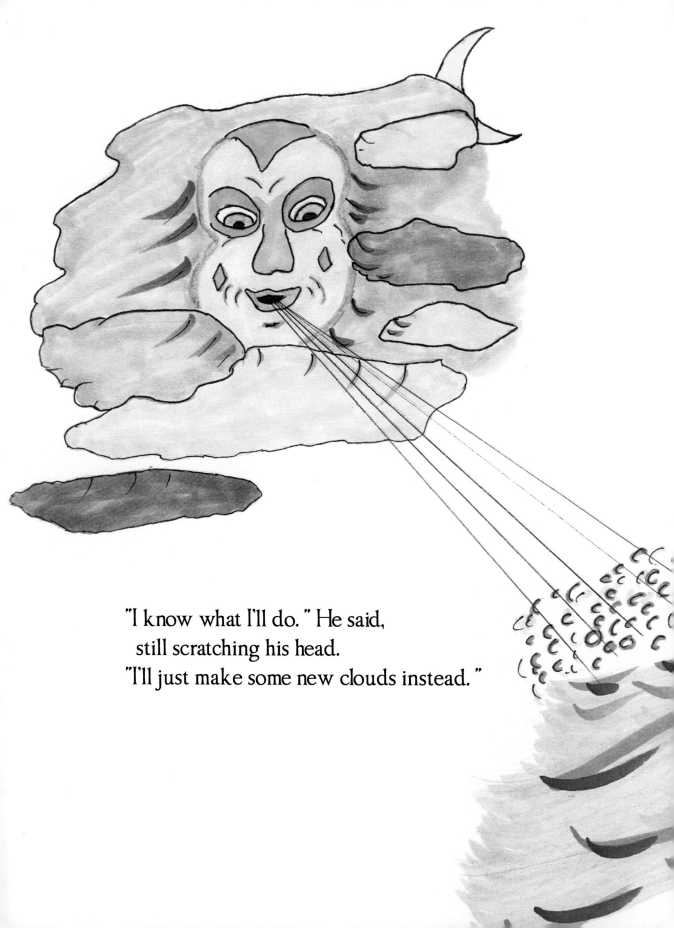

"I know what I'll do." He said,
  still scratching his head.
"I'll just make some new clouds instead."

So he looked out over
the wide ocean blue
and he blew the wildest wind
you ever knew.

The rain dance ended.
Everyone went home to their beds.
But they still had the hummmm,
of that drum, inside their heads.

Little Apple was dark
but still not wet.
It wasn't raining,
well, not yet.

And so McNat and Bungie Boo
went back to the old shed
that looked like a shoe.

They were wondering if
old Cloudius even knew.

Now, would he make it rain
or would he not?
He was getting so old,
he might have forgot.

So there you are and there you have it and that's what it's all about.

What happened after the Raindance?

Did it rain?

Watch out for the next rhyming stories:

Stories from Little Apple

The Little Apple stories are a collaboration by
Glenn McLernon and Lorraine Harvey

The Raindance:
First published in 2014 by Glenn McLernon.
Phone: 07503 184650 (UK)
E.mail: gmclernon@googlemail.com

The Raindance: Copyright© Glenn McLernon
Illustrations: Copyright© Glenn McLernon

ISBN: 978-0-9929145-0-9

A catalogue record of this book is available from the British Library.